# THE GEM OF TAGATH

# THE GEM OF TAGATH

## A TESHOVAR NOVELLA

JASON DOROUGH

This is a work of fiction. All the characters and events portrayed in this novel are fictitious.

THE GEM OF TAGATH

A 908 Press Book

ISBN eBook 978-1-7366140-2-0
ISBN Paperback 978-1-7366140-4-4

Esterburgh

Karsk

Aramore

Tresa

Ordport

Ornamen

Salkire

Deakem

Gramery

Klubridge

Bria

Craydon

Redwater

Trowood

Rifast

Teusas

Lakeband

Sandwallow

Dushouca

Acleau

Inport

Plier Gleau

MADIGUS SEA

Meskia

W · E

S

TESHOVAR

TO ORDPORT

TO DEAKEM

NORTHGARDEN

KLUBRIDGE
COLLEGE

THEATER
DISTRICT

CITY
CENTER

HENBURN
ESTATE

PORT

FINANCIAL
QUARTER

CANDLESTICK

MIDTOWN
CROSS

O GRAMERY

THE
DOWNSTEPS

EAST
WARD

TO REDWATER

City of
Klubridge

# THE GEM OF TAGATH

# CHAPTER 1

Pria's pulse quickened, and her fingers tightened on the cane. It was dark where she was standing with Cricket, hidden in the shadowy alcove. She'd already had the smaller boy shimmy up the lamppost and extinguish the streetlight that would have given them away. Now they stood in the black and empty street, peering around the corner at the ramshackle house.

"This it? You sure?" Cricket hissed, crouched next to Pria with his impossibly skinny legs bent and his knobby knees poking upward. His shaggy brown hair hung over his forehead and covered his eyes so he kept having to blow it out of the way.

"It's where Barween said," she whispered back and glanced down. At thirteen, Cricket was only two years younger than Pria was, but he barely came up to her shoulders when he was standing at full height.

Pria sniffed and made herself stop tapping the metal

tip of the cane against the uneven paving. Nerves or excitement. She wasn't sure which, so she focused on the house.

The building leaned to the left, away from its neighbors, and looked ready to collapse at a breath. Pria was used to seeing places like this in the East Ward, but it was more unusual toward the Downsteps. There wasn't any more money here than in the East Ward, but somehow the houses held up better. Not this one, though. Not Therron Bel's house.

"He home?" Lump had finally caught up with them, and his breathing came loud and heavy. His threadbare shirt stuck to his belly with sweat even though it wasn't a warm night, and his thick cheeks were shiny in the moonlight.

Pria looked up at the taller boy. "How should I bleeding know?" But it was a fair question. She couldn't see any light coming from inside either of the cracked windows that flanked the front door. Everything was dark, but that didn't mean anything. "Let's go find out, yeah?"

Lump shuffled his feet and looked down at them. "Coulda been here sooner with proper shoes."

"Want me around back?" Cricket asked. "Case if they make a run for it?"

Pria hesitated but shook her head. "You and Lump stick with me. Don't need you running off." She didn't need him running off, but she also didn't need him sneaking in the back and swiping the money for himself while she and Lump were trying to get in the front. Pria didn't know whether Cricket would do that, but she could throw the scrawny little wretch a good bit farther than she trusted him.

Cricket frowned. "It's just, what if he tries to get out the back way, see?"

"No," she snapped back at him, and that would be the end of it. He should know by now when she'd had the final word. Pria waited a moment in the silence and was satisfied when Cricket gave no further argument. "Now," she said, "we go in the front. You two back me up, compre?"

"Compre," the boys said in unison, and the plan was set.

Pria tugged on the brim of her hat and pulled it down closer to her eyebrows. She slid her fingers along the front and slipped out of the alcove and around the corner, careful to lift the cane so it wouldn't rattle on the street. She didn't need to look back to know the other two were following. Cricket's furtive scurrying and Lump's heavy stride were unmistakable.

When they reached the front of the house, Pria tried the doorknob. Locked. She stepped aside and jerked her head toward the door. "Do it, big boy."

Lump took a breath before launching himself hard against the door. Pria was a little surprised it withstood that first bash. The rest of the house looked like rotten kindling, but the door was sturdier stuff. Lump took a step back and went at the door again. He grunted when his shoulder bashed into it this time, and the wood around the lock splintered. The door slammed inward, and Lump's momentum carried him into the house with it.

Pria rounded the corner fast behind him with Cricket in her wake. She took in the room with a quick sweep of her eyes. It was bright with lamplight, after all. The windows were just blacked out with boards and black fabric from the inside. A man with curly gray hair had been sitting on a stool at a table to the right of the room, and he was halfway up, startled, as they barged in.

"I don't have anything!" he was shouting, his hands raised in front of him.

"Oh, that's where you're wrong, Therron Bel." Pria hopped onto the table and kicked a foot onto his shoulder. She shoved him back onto the stool, a little rougher than necessary. That's the only way they'd know you were serious.

He was sitting again now, his eyes jumping from one of them to another, but they came back to Pria, and she saw fear there. Pria squatted on the table in front of him, and Bel dropped his gaze. He knew who was in charge. "Barween Drach sent you."

"First try right," Pria said and stuck the knob of her cane under his chin to raise his face to meet her eyes. "You owe her. Where is it?"

"I need more time," he whimpered. "Please."

Pria clucked her tongue. "The boys and me didn't come all the way out here for nothing. Barween knows you got the seri today. She got ears and eyes where you don't even know. Now, tell me where it is, and we all go home nice, yeah?"

Bel shook his head but wouldn't look her in the eye. "I just don't have—"

Pria shoved the cane's knob hard into his throat, and he toppled backwards off the stool. He'd barely had time to hit the floor on his back when she was already over him, her foot planted on his chest. "That ain't what we like to hear, is it?"

"No," Cricket said. He was around the table and looking down at Bel now, beside Pria.

Bel had his hands up again, palms toward them. "You don't need to do this. How old are you kids?"

"Fourteen," Lump mumbled.

"Lump, shut up," Pria said over her shoulder, not taking her eyes off the man on the ground. And then, to Bel, "You got one more chance. Where's the seri?"

He said nothing, but his eyes flicked to the right for just an instant, toward the back of the house. Toward the door Pria hadn't bothered with until now. Her head snapped to face it just in time to see a frightened woman's eye in the open crack an instant before the door slammed shut and a bolt shot home.

Lump was already heading toward it, his shoulder down. This one took three hits to bash open, and when it finally gave way, Pria felt her stomach turn cold. She was staring through a second room, presently empty, that gave way to the back door of the house, now standing open and abandoned. The woman had taken the seri and run.

"Listen," Therron Bel was saying from the floor, "tell Barween—"

Pria swung her cane and cut him off with a sharp crack to the side of his skull. Not enough to finish him, but enough to quiet him and leave him with a reminder. Nothing he could have told her to tell Barween Drach would help with this situation. If that woman didn't turn up with the missing money, and fast, somebody would be fishing Bel out of the Klubridge sewers. Might be fishing Pria out, too, if she didn't play this right. Barween wasn't going to be happy.

# CHAPTER 2

B arween wasn't happy.

Pria stood facing the woman, the two of them in Barween's office with only a desk between them. Cricket was silent, standing far behind Pria and likely hoping that distance would save him from the gangster's wrath. Barween had been sitting but was standing now, not that it made much difference for her height. She was short and wide, and Pria knew Barween's dark muscles were thick, hidden beneath the layers of patterned and patched fabric wrapped around her. That night she had a multicolored turban holding back her wild hair that still was mostly black but had started running through with gray streaks.

"This is a joke, yes? Something to make Barween laugh." She tossed her head back. "Ho ho ho, see? Barween laughs at this." There was no mirth in that laugh, though, nor in the frown she gave Pria following it. "Now that you have had your fun, you will speak truth to Barween."

"It's the truth," Pria said and forced herself to meet the woman's gaze. She felt herself trying to look down like Therron bleeding Bel had done when he was afraid earlier, but she was not afraid of Barween Drach. Definitely not. "We went in the house, see, and somebody took off out the back with the seri. A woman."

Barween squinted at her and chewed at the inside of her cheek before speaking. "Who is this woman?"

"I don't know. A friend of Bel's, maybe? His wife?"

"Fah!" Barween waved her hand dismissively, and Pria managed not to flinch. "Therron Bel has no wife, no husband, no friend. Therron Bel has drink and debt."

"I don't know who she was, but she was there, in the back room. Saw us and bolted the door. By the time Lump got it open, she was gone out the back and disappeared."

"Gone where? A woman does not just disappear. Unless she were a mage. Were she a mage, Pria?" Barween gave a mocking gasp. Of course the woman hadn't been a mage.

"Cricket went after her one way, and I went the other. Weren't a sign of her, though. I'm—" Pria was about to apologize, but that's not what you did with Barween Drach. You got things right, or you didn't. And if you didn't already have them right, then you'd damned well better make them right. Apologies were

8

no currency here. "I'm going to make it right," she finished.

"Make it right, fah. Did no one think to watch the back door?"

"I did," Cricket said. Pria had nearly forgotten he was in the room. "Pria said Lump and me was to back her up, and she didn't want me running off. So that's what we did."

Pria could have strangled the little wretch in that moment, but she kept her face smooth. Everything was dice. Just keep breathing, and she'd be fine.

Barween raised an eyebrow at Pria but spoke to Cricket. "Pria needs no backup from you, little stick. She thought you'd sneak in the back and take the money yourself. She has no trust for you."

"I'd never—" Cricket started, but Barween hushed him with a sharply raised finger.

"Pria has no trust for any," Barween said. "Isn't that right?"

Pria had to say something, but she refused to give Barween the satisfaction of admitting she was right. Pria pinched her lips together and breathed through her nose for a long moment. "I trust myself. That's what you need in the end, yeah?"

Barween clucked and gave her the hint of a smile. "Trust yourself. Listen to you, a little girl trusting herself." She came around the desk and poked a thick and stubby finger into Pria's chest. "This? This not enough. Not if you want to make something of yourself. You have to trust others, too. Cricket, you trust Pria?"

"I... I guess so." He sounded uncertain, but Pria knew that was just fear. Cricket and Lump would follow her off the top of the Imperial tower if she told them to.

"See?" Barween said and hooked her finger under one of Pria's suspenders and snapped it back, hard. "Trust." She crossed her arms and let the swirling patterns on her long sleeves hang loose over her belly. "Now you tell Barween how you going to make this right."

"Therron Bel," Pria said. "After the woman ran out, I knocked him cold. We brought him back here. Lump's got him outside all trussed up with twine."

"Therron Bel does not have Barween's money. What good is this man? You think you make it right to give Barween the pleasure of crunching his bones? Is that it?"

"No. Well, yes. You can crunch his bones, but I'd wager his bones mean more to him than that woman does. Crunch him enough, and he'll tell you who she is. Where she went."

"And then what? Barween sends you after the seri again? Barween trusts you?" She emphasized that last bit and smirked at Pria.

Pria had no answer. Either this would work or it wouldn't. If it didn't, Pria wasn't likely to be around long enough to worry about it.

Barween took a step back and tapped her finger

against her lower lip. "Okay. Yes, this is what will happen. Because Barween has decided to trust you one more time."

Pria hadn't realized she'd been holding her breath until she exhaled. She could work with this.

But Barween was still talking. "Trust," she said again. "That is what bought you another chance. You see the value? You trust, and you move ahead. Remember this."

"Yes, Barween," Pria said, and then she was out of the office and making a fast shuffle to the front door, with Cricket close behind her. They passed countless supplicants and lackeys sprawled through the building, some of them playing cards, some standing at attention with their hands on knives, and still others drugged out of their minds and rolling around in the corners.

Cricket was trying to talk to her as they moved through the rooms of the dimly lit hideout, his voice a raspy whisper. "Sorry, Pria. I didn't mean to get her after you like—"

"Shush," Pria snapped back. This wasn't the time for that. She'd deal with him later, after they were well away from Barween Drach and her creepy legion of followers.

Lump was waiting outside where she'd left him, one of his big hands wrapped around Therron Bel's shoulder. Bel sat on the street, his back propped against the outside of Barween's hideout. They had bound him at the wrists and ankles, with a fair amount of twine wrapped around the rest of him for good measure. He was awake by now, and his eyes were big and terrified.

"Don't give me to her. Please. You know what she'll do," he begged. He tried to raise his hands to plead, but they were secured too tightly for him to get farther than a weak twitch.

Pria ignored the man and nodded to Lump. "Toss him inside and tell one of Barween's people who he is. They'll know what to do with him."

Lump hoisted Bel over his shoulder with no effort and started through the door. He paused before going in and told Pria, "Something going on at Henburn."

"What is it?" she asked.

"Dunno. Something strange," he said and disappeared through the doorway.

The Henburn Estate was at the center of Klubridge, up all the way through Candlestick and out the other side. It was a fair distance from here in the East Ward, but he'd raised her curiosity.

"We going to see?" Cricket asked.

"I go. You stay here. Make sure Lump does what he's supposed to."

Cricket looked disappointed but didn't argue. He rarely did. Pria watched him go back in the door before she turned left and headed uptown.

The City Center was fancier than down here. Pria was glad to be wearing her suspenders today, and her green hat as well. She didn't try and fool herself into thinking she could blend with that kind of crowd, but she might stand out a little less. She gave her cane a little toss from one hand to the other. Having the cane added some class, too. Every little bit helped. Maybe she could steal a monocle, too, one day.

One day. One day she wouldn't have to be thieving off the streets. She'd be running her own gang, and she'd do a better job of it than Barween Drach or Mascon or Scrounger or any of those old fools who thought they ran Klubridge. She wouldn't make mistakes like they did. She wouldn't let the others keep at their petty schemes like Barween did. One day Pria would run the whole show, and the rest of them would make way for her or get their own cracks in the head. She liked that and gave her cane a little spin.

A lot of work and the right kind of plotting would get her there. But trust? That's the last thing she needed. Trust got you a knife in the back, no matter what Barween might be going on about. Maybe she could make sure Barween got her own knifing. One day.

But on this day, Pria was through Candlestick and coming into the City Center. The castle at the middle of the Henburn Estate was ahead of her, angled up the sloping hill, and the Imperial tower stood massive at its center, the tallest thing in all of Klubridge. Tallest thing she'd ever seen, in truth. There were people standing around in the street, gawking up at something, no matter that it was nearly the middle of the night.

Pria had to squint to see it, but then she did, dark against the white stone and ornamentation of the tower wall, the very tower she'd been thinking about earlier while in Barween's office. Even though it was nighttime, that tower always stood out bright in the moonlight.

"There's something you don't see every day," she said, and it was true. It wasn't every day you could spot a person midway up the side of the Imperial tower, dead and strung up by his neck.

# CHAPTER 3

The body on the tower was a sensation that night and into the following morning, but Klubridge forgot about it as soon as the guards cut it down. It was a petty thief the City Watch strung up as a warning to the gangs, according to some. It was a mage and a traitor to the High Lord the Kites strung up as a warning to the rebels, according to others. Pria thought whatever the message was hadn't been clear enough, and nobody really knew who was up on that tower, only that the Empire had put him there. In any case, the body was gone now, and she had other problems on her mind. Chief among them was whether Barween's thugs could get any information out of Therron Bel.

Bel had been at Barween's place for a full day by now, and there had been no word. Pria sat on the edge of a rooftop only a block away and scrubbed paint onto a second-story wall while she fretted over the situation. Painting was what she did when she had worries. She didn't think she was very good at it, but she was prolific, with all the worrying she did as one of Barween Drach's favorite little runners.

Nobody thought this twig of a girl with dirty, pale skin and stringy, dark yellow hair was a threat until she was laying her cane into the side of their head. Bel found out about that, and Pria was pretty sure she'd cracked his temple with that swing when he was on the floor. His temple was the least of her worries, though. He needed to tell where that woman had gone, and Pria needed to get that money back. If she didn't, she was familiar with how Barween dealt with her own worries.

Pria dipped a rag into the blue paint and smeared the color over the brickwork. It was nighttime again, but she could see well enough by the light of the moon. The colors always looked a little different in the daytime, but all she cared about was how they looked after the sun was down.

Some red now, and she caught herself scrawling out her name in big, block symbols. It was the only word she knew how to write. She stared at the first two letters before continuing with the last two. So what if people knew she was the one painting up the walls all around the East Ward? So much the better. They'd all know her name soon enough, anyway.

She'd just finished with the red and was about to outline the letters in white when movement down below caught her eye. The street had been quiet that night, especially around this part of the Ward, but there was someone on the move down there, creeping about slower than she liked. Pria leaned out from the roof and peered down. It was a girl, around her own age, maybe a little younger. Definitely younger. What was she up to?

Pria grabbed her hat from where she'd stowed it next to the paints and shoved it onto her head before she slipped her legs over the edge and dropped off the roof. She landed in a crouch on the pavement, being careful to raise her cane so it didn't bang against the ground and snap.

"Ey!" she called, and the girl flinched in the middle of the street. She looked toward Pria but couldn't see her, where she had landed in the building's shadow. Pria stepped out into the moonlight and let the younger girl get a look at her. "What you doing here, squeak?"

From down here, Pria could see that the girl was indeed a little younger, maybe by a year, but not much. She was a little shorter than Pria, too, and thin, but not as rail skinny as Pria. And, like Pria, this girl had yellow hair, but hers looked lighter and cleaner. Pria reached to touch her own hair but caught herself and adjusted her hat's brim instead. "Who are you?"

The girl took a step back from Pria, but not entirely out of fear. It was a smart step, positioning her so she was farther out of reach of the cane if Pria took a notion to swing at her. "I'm here to see Barween Drach," the girl said. "My name's Fairy."

"Fairy," Pria said and laughed. It was a ridiculous name, but most of the kids here had as bad or worse. Pria still had her own birth name and unfortunately remembered her own parents, but most of the rest hadn't been so lucky. Fairy didn't have as bad a name as Lump, she supposed. "What business do you have with Barween, eh?"

Fairy looked uncertain then. She glanced down the street in the direction she'd been walking, toward Barween's hideout. She knew her way around. "What I've got to say is just for Barween."

Pria walked out into the street, closing the distance between herself and Fairy, and she dragged the cane behind her, letting the metal tip rattle across the hard roadway. Sometimes she could get it to strike a spark if it hit just the right kind of stone at the right angle. No spark this time, and Fairy held her ground but kept an eye on the cane. Sturdy girl, used to this life, but she didn't look mean enough for it. "Who you with?" Pria asked her.

"With?"

"You're from here in the Ward, yeah? But I don't know you."

Fairy studied her for a long moment. "I need to see—"

"You need to see Barween. I heard you. I work for Barween, and this is as close as you're getting to her this night. If I let you go the rest of the way you were heading, you wouldn't be coming back. Now," Pria said, "what you want?"

Fairy looked down the street one more time but didn't make a move to head that way. She looked back at Pria. "I'm with Scrounger's gang. East of here."

"I know where he is."

"One of Scrounger's boys was in this area last night. He got beaten badly. I need to find out who did it."

Pria managed not to laugh, only because the answer was so far away from anything she expected. "And you, what? You expect Barween bleeding Drach to tell you which one of her boys put a beating on yours? Come off it. You'd be the next one with a beating."

Fairy squared her shoulders and turned up her chin. "I'm asking you, then. Who beat him up?"

"How should I know? And who is this boy, anyway? He your boyfriend or something?"

Fairy's nose wrinkled, and that was when Pria decided she liked this girl. Fairy said, "Skink is not my boyfriend, and that's a fact. He's not even a friend, truly."

"So you want to revenge him? That it? Because he's another one of Scrounger's rats?"

Fairy sighed and looked at Pria. Really looked at her for the first time. "Are you going to help me or not?"

"Leaning toward not, but I could be persuaded."

"I just need to know who did it and where they are. Could you find that out?"

Now Pria was looking at Fairy. What was this really about? This Fairy seemed more practical than flying off just to get revenge for a beating on a boy she didn't even like. There was something she wasn't saying.

"Did your boy get robbed?"

Fairy stared back, and her eyes narrowed. "They might have taken a few seri."

"And you want it back?"

"Maybe."

But this wasn't about some seri. There was something more valuable here. Something that boy lost and that Fairy needed to get back. Maybe this was a play from Scrounger himself. Pria smelled opportunity.

"Let's say I keep an eye out," Pria said. "I let you know if I hear anything, yeah?"

"You know where to find me, compre?"

"Compre."

"All right, then." Fairy stood there for another breath before she turned and went back the way she'd come.

Pria would have an eye out, all right, but she wouldn't be sharing what she found with any of Scrounger's brats. Fairy was looking for something valuable enough to have her out to meet Barween Drach in the middle of the night. Whatever it was, Pria would find it, and it wouldn't end up in the hands of Scrounger or Barween or any of the rest of them. This was hers, and she didn't need anyone else to make it happen.

# CHAPTER 4

Therron Bel talked on the third day of his captivity, and it took Pria and her boys less than two hours to track down his sister west of Candlestick, near the Midtown Cross. The less said about that, the better. No more than an hour after that, Pria dropped the satchel full of money on Barween's desk.

"We dice now?" she asked, knowing the answer but needing to hear it anyway.

Barween weighed the bag in her hands and jangled the coins inside. "Oh no, we not dice, miss. You just finished what you started for Barween three nights ago. We never dice, though."

Pria sniffed and nodded, and she was halfway out of the office when Barween called at her back, "And you'd best stop marking up buildings. Barween has told you how many times?"

She stopped at the door and half turned back to Barween. "Several times."

The older woman clucked her tongue and shook a finger at her. "You best start listening to Barween. Go now."

So Pria went. There would be no advancing in Barween Drach's gang, and there would be no respect from Barween, even when a job was done and done well. But that wasn't what Pria was thinking about now.

She'd been doing what she told Fairy she'd do. Her eyes were open, and her ears were open, but more than that, she'd been asking around. Not in the dull and obvious way Fairy had done, making herself into bait. No, Pria knew the East Ward, and she knew how to get people to tell her things without them even realizing it. Fairy might live here, but she didn't seem like she'd seen enough of the streets to know how to use them.

Whatever that boy had lost, Pria was going to get it.

It hadn't been any of Barween's lot that beat the boy, that much was sure. She'd also ruled out Mascon's gang after snooping on some of his street runners. They didn't do that sort of thing anyway, and neither did Scrounger. He had his kids into pickpocketing and running minor scams. They weren't muscle, and there'd have been no sense in beating and robbing their own boy. That didn't leave many options in the Ward, and Pria felt sure she knew where to look.

Kam Dhaz didn't run with children like most of the other gangs of Klubridge. Kids were easy to manipulate. They didn't have their own agendas, and they were too afraid and too stupid to intentionally go against their masters. And it was just as easy to disavow and abandon children when they got caught. Adults were harder to manage, but there was no doubt they were more effective.

All of Dhaz's people were grownups. Pria had seen them stalking the streets many a night, and she'd stumbled across more than one mugging where they'd beaten some poor fool senseless before rifling through their pockets once they were unconscious. That's the type of work Kam Dhaz was into, and Pria knew his gang wouldn't shy away from pummeling one of Scrounger's boys, given good reason.

After leaving Barween with Therron Bel's money, Pria confirmed her suspicion by slipping a handful of coins out of a newsboy's pocket and later shifting them into the dirty palm of one of Dhaz's underlings. The man was dark and short and hunched, his back curved from birth, but Pria saw strength in those hands and cunning in his black eyes.

"Aye, it was Melemander what beat the boy. He'd come trying to sell something to Kam. You know how that go."

Pria didn't know, but she surmised the answer and nodded. "What was he selling, then?"

"Don't know that, but I do know Mele got it for a discount and brung it back to Kam. Paid the boy in knuckles, not seri." The man chuckled at that.

"So Kam Dhaz has whatever it was now?"

He huffed and shoved Pria's shoulder. "Maybe he do, maybe he don't. That's not for me to worry over, nor for you." He shook his pocket with the seri she'd given him. "That's as far as your payment gets you, girl. I'm done with you now."

Except that he wasn't done with her, or rather she wasn't done with him. Pria doubled back after she was out of sight of the man, and she took to the roofs, following him all the way to the northern edge of the East Ward, nearly as far as Candlestick. It was a better area of Klubridge but still fell well beneath the interest of the ne'er-do-wells that spent their time still farther north and west in the city. Nobody of any importance would notice the nondescript building where the hunched man ended up that evening, especially with no sort of sign or identifying marks on it. It looked like just another abandoned shop in a neighborhood full of bankrupt businesses.

But Pria knew better. She had an eye for details and noted the heavy metal door at the front with a large housing for its lock. She also studied the windowless walls on both sides of the structure, no other ways in or out, as far as she could tell, and no single bit of decay or dilapidation on the building. This place was sturdy, and it was being taken care of. It looked too small to be a proper base of operations, but it had to be one of Kam Dhaz's properties. There had to be something worth protecting in there.

Pria should have been back at Barween's by full dark, and she knew Cricket and Lump would be looking for her, but she stayed in place on that rooftop across from Dhaz's building. She had watched the man she paid wait outside the building, propped next to an empty little vendor stall, for nearly two hours. But then someone else came, a woman he seemed to recognize. She wore a cloak with the hood pulled up, barely hiding her dark hair. The man slid something out of his jacket and handed it to her. She took it to that big metal door and stood there until the man hobbled around and into the thing Pria had thought was a vendor stall. But now she could see it was built into the front of the building and was as much a part of the structure as the wall behind it.

From her vantage point, Pria could see the man stepping carefully onto what looked like a metal square in the booth's floor and standing there while the woman turned a key in the lock in the door. That done, the man pulled a lever in front of him, hidden from the view of the street but in plain sight from above, where Pria was perched. She heard a loud clang as the locks disengaged, and the metal door swung open. The woman went inside, stayed for just a moment, and came back out without whatever the man had given her. He stepped out of the booth, and the door to the building closed of its own accord. Without a word to each other, they went their separate ways.

When she was sure they had gone, Pria climbed down to the road and crossed to the strange building. It was just short of midnight by then, but she could see well enough to examine the metal door and its lock before going to the booth where the man had pulled the lever. Just as she thought, there was a metal plate built into the floor of the little booth. Pria pressed on it with her palm first, and then tested it with her foot. It shifted down and came back up when she moved off it, but nothing else happened. She tried tugging on the lever, and it wouldn't budge.

Then she tried pressing on the metal plate with her foot while pulling on the lever. At first, the lever remained stuck, but then it shifted just a hair. She grunted and pressed harder on the plate, leveraging her weight down by pressing her back against the wall as her feet pushed down. Pria grunted with the effort. For an instant, the lever actually moved, pulling down toward her, and then stopping as she pressed even harder on the plate.

Pria bit at her lip and stepped back to examine the setup. This was engineering beyond anything an East Ward gang should have been able to manage. The lever moved only when she depressed the plate, but not always. Only when she pressed the plate in a certain way. She suspected finding the right way to press the plate and pulling that lever at the same time was Kam Dhaz's overly complicated way of opening that big door, and it only would happen after someone else turned the key in the big lock. Who had built this for him?

She looked back and forth from the lock on the door to the booth with the lever. This wasn't something she could do on her own, after all. She could pull

Lump or Cricket into the scheme, but this couldn't get back to Barween, and she didn't trust them enough to keep their mouths shut around the others. Pria wiped a weary hand over her face. It was time to find Fairy again.

# CHAPTER 5

P ria had told Fairy she knew where Scrounger's hideout was, but the truth was that she'd never been there. She vaguely knew its general placement in the East Ward, but it wasn't hard to pinpoint once she set out to find it the day after she'd discovered Kam Dhaz's locked door. She followed a gaggle of filthy urchins running through the streets of the East Ward after she spotted them convening at a crossroads. Pria had seen one of them lift a wallet off an unsuspecting laborer not two minutes earlier, and now they were in the wind, headed back to their hovel.

And what a hovel it was. The East Ward was a poor and dangerous area to begin with, but Scrounger had based his operations in the absolute slums of the Ward. His hideout was in a decrepit building that was in even worse shape than Therron Bel's house had been, and that was saying something. All the houses on that street stood in various states of disrepair, and the whole place had a feeling of abandonment Pria never had felt near Barween's headquarters. There always were thieves and scoundrels coming and going at Barween's, but this place had the stillness of death after the little cutpurses Pria was following disappeared into the darkness of the front door. Some kind of rough fabric hanging covered the doorway, and they had to push it aside and duck to get in.

Pria leaned against the corner of a building diagonal from Scrounger's den and watched that doorway for a few minutes. Fairy might or might not be in there. It was early evening now, the time when the little cretins would be ranging out and lifting seri from anybody dumb enough to make themselves a target. Fairy had given Pria the impression that she didn't get out on the streets much, so she might not emerge from that door tonight.

"Oy," a rough and nasal voice called. Watching the door had made her miss the boy slipping up on her right side. Sloppy. "What you want, then?"

The boy was just a little shorter than Pria and had tangled hair that looked like mice had slept in it. His left eye was swollen shut and purple, and somebody had bruised up his nose as well. He was breathing through his mouth, and Pria saw his teeth were foul, and more than a few were missing.

"Looks like you had a fun time of it," she said.

He reached up to the side of his face and winced when his fingers touched near his eye. "What of it? Who're you anyway?"

"You must be Skink."

He'd been taking another step toward her, but that halted him. "How you know that?" His good eye darted around. "I mean, if that's who I be."

"I heard there's an ugly orphan named Skink down here who got his arse beat the other night. Sound retto?"

Now he was coming toward her again, his face squinty and angry the way Lump got when somebody insulted him. Pria raised her cane and stopped him with the tip against his chest. "Far enough, you. You didn't just catch a beating, did you? You also lost your cargo. Retto?"

This put him off balance again, and he studied Pria before shooting a glance at the door to Scrounger's hideout. "Who told you that?"

"Nobody had to tell me." Pria leaned toward him, over her extended cane, and showed some of her own teeth, none missing, thank you. "I know things."

Skink stepped back so the cane wasn't pushing into his chest, and he looked toward the hideout again. "You ain't getting me in trouble, yeah?"

She pretended to think about it for a moment before lowering the cane and saying, "Might be we can work something out. You know a girl called Fairy?"

He blinked, and his attention was back on Pria. "Fairy? What you want with her?"

"She in there?" Pria jerked her head in the direction Skink had been looking.

"Maybe. Why?"

"You go get her for me without letting anybody else know. Tell her to come to that alley," Pria said, pointing. "I'll be waiting. You do that, nobody needs to hear about how you lost your treasure."

The boy shuffled his feet and swallowed. He finally stepped away from Pria and into the street, but kept his eyes on her. "You ain't telling nobody." And then he was gone, under the heavy fabric and into the blackness of the hideout.

Pria rounded the corner into the alley she'd indicated but didn't go so far into it that she couldn't see the door from where she waited. She'd put the fear into Skink for certain, but she wasn't confident he was smart enough to remember where he was to send Fairy. It was only another moment or two before the fabric pulled back, and Pria saw a familiar blond head duck under it. Fairy emerged into the evening and looked up and down the street before crossing directly to Pria's alley.

"I thought it might be you," she said when she saw Pria lurking next to a rotting wooden crate. "What did you tell Skink? He looked ready to cry."

"I told him he'd send you out, or I'd let Scrounger know about what he lost when he got his beating."

Fairy pursed her lips and appraised Pria. "And what is it that he lost?"

"I don't know, but it's something valuable enough to have you both worried and to have the person who stole it locking it up tight."

Fairy's eyes widened. "You found it! Who was it?"

"Tsk, tsk, not just yet. First you tell me what it is, and then I tell you how we can get it."

"We?"

"It's a two-person job, and I might volunteer myself if you can interest me with the next thing you say."

Fairy took her time in responding, no doubt debating whether she could trust Pria. Of course Fairy couldn't trust her, but Pria was betting she wouldn't realize that, or at least would be desperate enough to bend a little. Pria was right.

"It's the Gem of Tagath."

Pria was expecting a lot of responses, but that wasn't one of them. She barked a laugh, louder than she'd meant to, and clapped a hand over her mouth before saying, "And I'm the bleeding High Lord Peregrine. Try again, this time with the truth."

"It's the truth. My friend lifted it and didn't even know what he had until he got back the other night. I guess an Imperial messenger was passing through with it. He was in disguise. Dorrin couldn't have known who he was robbing."

Pria was about to object again, but she saw sincerity in Fairy's eyes. "One of the Imperial jewels is coming through Klubridge, and your mate just happens to steal it by accident."

"It is what it is. It's the truth. You could ask the messenger if they hadn't hanged him off the side of the tower at Henburn."

A second of silence passed between the girls before

Pria admitted, "I saw him. They cut him down shortly after."

Fairy nodded. "So now, how do we get it back? Who has it?"

"You're best leaving that thing gone, Fairy. How do you expect to pawn an Imperial gem? The City Watch'll be all over Klubridge looking for the bleeding thing. All over the Ward, sure."

"Scrounger said the same thing. I'm not going to sell it. That's what Skink tried to do. After he saw Scrounger wasn't planning to do anything with the gem, he swiped it and snuck out. That's when he got beaten and lost it. Scrounger hasn't seen it's gone yet, and I intend for it to be exactly where he left it the next time he goes to check."

"And you don't want him murdering Skink."

"I couldn't care less about him. It's the rest of us I worry about. When Scrounger takes it out on one of us, the others usually catch it as well. And this would be a big one."

Pria understood. Barween tended to be more specific with her wrath, but it wasn't uncommon for that to spill over with some collateral damage. "What does he plan to do with the thing, anyway?"

"How should I know? He just put it in his office, hidden away. Maybe he's gonna keep it there. It's just a stupid gem. The point is, it needs to get back there. Are you going to help me now?"

Of course, it was anything but just a stupid gem. Pria knew all about the Gem of Tagath and the nonsense people believed about it, but it was clear that Fairy didn't. She kept her breathing even and adjusted her hat before answering. "I'll help you. It was one of Kam Dhaz's runners what took it. I can show you where he's got it. We'll have to work together to get it back from him."

Fairy's eyebrows rose when she heard the name Kam Dhaz, but she gave Pria a firm nod. "Partners, then. Let's go get it."

# CHAPTER 6

"We're going to need that key," Fairy whispered.

This time it was a thin man with long hair at the door. He followed the routine the same as Pria had seen on her own and the same as the two of them had seen just an hour earlier. After the long-haired man disengaged the main lock, the stocky woman in the booth pulled on the lever, and the door ratcheted open.

"What you think?" Pria asked, looking down from the top of the building where she'd first spotted this process. "Pickpocket him?"

Fairy shook her head. "I don't know. We can't take it any way he'd know it was missing. He'd come straight back here and find us."

"What, then? Replace it with a fake key?"

"Maybe. But we'd need something similar enough to convince him if he took a look in his pocket."

"I couldn't see it clear enough from up here," Pria said. "You?"

"No," Fairy said. "And what about the lever? That needs to be pulled after the key's in the lock."

"And it won't pull unless you're pressing down on the plate in the floor at the same time."

"What plate?"

"There's a metal plate, square like. I went down and pushed on it myself."

Fairy chewed on her lip. "It's to make sure whoever's pulling that lever is standing in the booth and stays there. One person inside and one person outside." She looked at Pria. "What happens if she steps off the plate or lets go of the lever while he's inside?"

"I imagine the door closes again."

"And then whoever's inside gets stuck there."

Pria hadn't thought about that twist. She'd been trying to decide who would be in the booth and who would go in the door. She was thinking about having Fairy in the booth so she couldn't run off with the treasure, but this changed her mind. Fairy would be the one to go in and retrieve the gem. As she thought about it, the thin man came back out the door, and now he had a small packet in his hand. Once he was clear of the door, the woman released the lever and stepped out to meet him. The door swung shut, just like Fairy had said.

"There's a special way to press the plate down, too," Pria said. "The lever won't pull unless you get it just right."

"How do you mean?"

"If you push it too gentle, nothing. Too hard, nothing. You have to get it pushed just right if you want that lever moving."

Fairy frowned and looked like she was trying to work out a puzzle. "So we need the key, and we need to find out the right way to step on that thing. The trick to it."

"That's not something we can pickpocket," Pria said.

"Reckon we could bribe one of them to show us?"

"Doubtful. What you got to give em that'd be worth them betraying Kam Dhaz to a couple of street rats?"

"I don't like this," Fairy said. "It's too complicated. We don't even know for sure that it's in there."

"The gem? Of course it is."

"Maybe it was, maybe not. Maybe it still is. But you've seen them coming and going, leaving some things and taking out others. This is a storehouse. A vault, maybe. It's where Kam Dhaz keeps his loot until he sells it."

Pria watched the pair below confer before they left in opposite directions, just like usual. The man was quick around the building, but the woman took her time, walking with a slight limp. "I think it's in there. I say it's worth trying."

"It's too risky. When would we even go in there? They're making pickups and deliveries all the time."

"Not during the daytime, they're not. They've only been coming after dark."

"So, what? We break into Kam Dhaz's vault in broad daylight?"

"Sure," Pria said, feeling the plan coming together. "We figure out the trick to the metal plate in the floor, and we swap out the key with one of Dhaz's people, and we get in."

"We don't even know what the key looks like," Fairy said. "You agreed, it was too far to see. We'd have to match the color, the shape. Even the weight would have to be perfect for what they feel in their pockets." She paused. "What?"

Pria's eyes were wide as the details fell into place. "That's it! The plate in the ground!" She looked at Fairy. "The three people I've watched go into that booth? They're all about the same size once you figure in how tall and how wide they are."

"You're saying the plate has to be pressed down by a particular weight? That's what makes the lever move?"

"And Dhaz hires the same size guards to stand on it. All the people who go in that booth weigh the same."

Fairy stared at Pria, looking like she was trying to find the flaw in the logic, but Pria knew she was right. Fairy finally shook her head. "We have no way of knowing what the key looks like for swapping it out, and now we have to weigh exactly the right amount to make that lever work. And, on top of that, the gem might not even be in there. Probably isn't, in fact."

"I'll wager it is," Pria said. "Just like we both said, you can't fence that thing. The City Watch's looking everywhere for that gem now. Kam Dhaz is many things, but a stupid dunk ain't one of them. He's like to hold on to it and lay low until the Watch moves on to some other crime. He'd keep it wherever's most secure, and I say we're looking at that place right now."

Fairy looked back down at the building in the darkness, and Pria knew she couldn't argue with the likelihood. She looked more afraid than doubtful now. "I still don't know. This isn't something I've done."

"What, then? You want to go back and get smacked around by Scrounger?"

Fairy ignored the question. "What's in this for you, anyway? Why are you helping me?"

Pria was surprised she hadn't asked that question sooner. "Taking Kam Dhaz down a peg's good for my reputation. I'll be running this city before long." That, and she wanted the gem in her own pocket.

It was hard to tell how much of the answer Fairy believed. She took her time studying Pria's face in the dark and finally shrugged. "How do we even do this, though?"

Pria cuffed her on the shoulder. "Listen to me. Here's how we do it."

# CHAPTER 7

The Skilled Lily was a tavern only a few blocks away from Kam Dhaz's vault. That's where following one of Dhaz's henchmen for the better part of the day took Pria and Fairy after they had stopped in at a candlemaker and then at an apothecary for quick purchases. Truth be told, Pria pocketed what she needed at the candlemaker without being seen, but she had to ask for help at the apothecary, and that had taken money.

The henchman was of average height, just a little pudgy, and with light brown skin. He wore a knitted sock hat pulled down to nearly his eyebrows, and it flopped at the side of his head as he made his rounds through the streets.

He stopped in at various shops and homes in the better part of the East Ward, and after an hour of that, Pria realized he was taking up protection collections. Kam Dhaz was shaking down the citizens in this part of the quarter. Absolutely repugnant, and something she'd have to remember to do when she ran things herself. After following him for a few hours, she heard one of his victims call him Tunkahl. Once Tunkahl had made all his collections and delivered all his threats, he guided his two shadows to the local bar.

Fairy asked with some trepidation, "We wait out here for him?"

"Nope," Pria said, leading the way. "We're going in."

Fairy lagged behind but eventually followed Pria and was right behind her by the time they reached the door. The tavern wasn't crowded yet. Drinkers and gamblers probably would pack it, come full nighttime, but now it was just late afternoon, and the only patrons were a few early arrivals in the corner. Pria spotted Tunkahl settling into a seat at an empty table to the left of the entrance, back in the corner.

"Come along," she whispered to Fairy and wove her way between the other tables and chairs to approach the man. He watched the two girls with suspicious eyes as they neared.

"Whatever it is, I don't want it," he said.

"Now, you haven't heard what it is," Pria said.

"Don't matter. I don't want it."

A young server with shrewd eyes was at the table now and glanced Pria's way before asking Tunkahl for his order. He told her he wanted ale, and she left with one more look at the girls. She didn't like seeing them hassling a paying customer.

Pria pulled out the chair across the table from

Tunkahl, turned it around backwards, and straddled it. She leaned over the low back of the chair, resting her arms atop it. "I say I can drink you under the table."

Tunkahl blinked at Pria and looked at Fairy, still standing behind her. "She daft?"

Fairy shrugged. "I just met her. I don't know. Maybe?"

He turned his attention back to Pria. "How old are you, little miss?"

"Fifteen," she said. She'd thought to lie like she usually did but went with the truth this time.

"And you think you can outdrink me, a fully growed man?"

"Fully growed, for certain," Pria said and mockingly patted her flat belly. "How much you weigh?"

"Enough to hold me drink," he snapped back.

"No, really, how much?"

"One ninety-three, if ye please. And ye look like a wind'd blow you away. You really think you want to challenge me."

"I don't think it." She pulled back her upper lip to give him what she knew was a wicked grin. "I know it."

The server had just returned and was placing Tunkahl's ale in front of him. "Let's see it, then," he said. And then, to the server, "Bring her one of the same."

Pria thought the woman might protest at her age, but she merely nodded and headed back to the bar.

"We going to make this interesting?" Tunkahl asked. "You got any seri on ye?"

Pria produced a coin from her right sleeve and dropped it on the table. "Better yet," she said, "let's make it five seri per mug."

"Per mug?" Tunkahl laughed and reached into his pocket for a coin. "Alright, girl, you've amused me. I'll watch you pass out midway through this drink, and I'll be leaving with your money. Your friend can watch and tell you later what a fool you made of yourself."

Pria put her hands together on the table and slipped two fingers into her left sleeve, where she had stowed the small white envelope from the apothecary. The server was back again and sat Pria's mug down with a hard thud. The ale sloshed, and a few drops spattered the table. Pria pinched a bit of powder out of the envelope and dropped it into her drink as she passed her hand over the top. Tunkahl didn't notice. If he didn't see her doctoring her own drink now, he certainly wouldn't notice it after she had him three or four rounds into this game.

Fairy saw it for sure, though, and she settled into the chair to Pria's right, giving her a meaningful and wide-eyed stare. "You want to join in?" Pria asked her.

Fairy frowned at her, and that was answer enough. Pria lifted the mug by the handle and raised it to Tunkahl. He chuckled and did the same before tipping his back and draining the ale in a few big gulps. Pria shook her mug lightly, giving the powder time to mix, and then started in on her drink. She wasn't able to down it as quickly as Tunkahl did, but she was close. She slammed the empty mug down a little harder than necessary and launched an enormous belch across the table at her rival.

"That's one," she said and flipped another coin onto the table.

Tunkahl watched the coin spin and settle, and then he dug another of his own out of his pocket. "All right, then." He waved to the server and called, "Two more." And then to Pria, "The loser pays for the drinks."

"Agreed," she said and settled back in her seat to await the next round of ale.

When it arrived, Pria pinched another bit of the powder into the mug. This time, she watched as it descended into the foul liquid. After a couple of seconds, it sparked and sizzled, too low for Tunkahl to see and hear it, but Pria knew what it was doing. She didn't know how it worked, of course, but she knew something in the powder reacted with the ale to super-heat and evaporate the alcohol. All that remained in the mug was a nasty-tasting swill that wouldn't get anyone drunk. Tunkahl didn't have that benefit.

Pria took the first gulp this time and finished her second drink in one long chug. She wiped at her mouth with the back of her hand while she watched Tunkahl finish his. That was two down, and Tunkahl wasn't swaying yet. He narrowed his eyes at her, and for an instant, she thought he was onto her. But no, he looked more impressed than suspicious.

"Two more!"

It went on like that for a third round, and then a fourth and a fifth followed. It had gotten dark outside, and Pria began to worry that she wouldn't have enough powder to see Tunkahl into unconsciousness. Tunkahl looked more surprised with each mug that neither he nor Pria showed any signs of drunkenness. Fairy got up from the table and wandered away after he called for the sixth round of ale.

Tunkahl leaned forward and studied Pria. "Where did you learn to drink, little bit?"

"Here and there," she said. "You seem to be holding your ale, too."

"I do," he said, "but it needs to get out somehow. I'll be back. Don't touch my seri."

Tunkahl pushed himself up from the table and headed for the door, and his lack of even a single staggered step dismayed Pria. How many mugs was she going to have to put into this man?

"Is he leaving?" Fairy asked, just then coming back to the table.

Pria shook her head. "After five mugs of ale, he's headed out for a piss. I can't say I won't be far behind, the way this is going."

"You're not going to get him drunk," Fairy said.

"Why not?"

"The barkeep. She's watering the drinks." Fairy glanced back toward the bar, where the woman even now was filling the sixth round. The bar had filled with patrons while they'd been drinking, so the service between each round had slowed down. "I was suspicious, so I watched her. There's not enough alcohol in what she's serving you to do anything to him."

Pria scowled and pulled the little white envelope out from her sleeve. "Looks like this was a waste, then."

"What do we do now?" Fairy asked.

"Follow me, and keep an eye out."

"For what?"

"Just follow me. And take the coins."

Fairy slid several of the five-seri marks off the table, but she left enough to cover the cost of the drinks. Pria rolled her eyes and scooped the rest of the money into her pocket. She then slapped her green hat back onto her head and grabbed her cane from where she'd propped it on the chair to her left. As the two girls moved toward the door, the server called after them, holding up the next two mugs.

"Pour it in your ear," Pria called back, and the rest of the bar roared in approval.

Pria shoved through the front door, and they were back out into the street. It was full dark by now, and she didn't know which way Tunkahl had gone. Fairy looked like she was going to ask something, but Pria shushed her with an upheld finger. She listened hard, and there it was: the sound of reconstituted ale hitting paving stones in a steady stream.

Pria nodded to the right and led Fairy around the corner of the tavern. It was even darker back there in the shadows of the neighboring buildings, but it was still light enough to see Tunkahl facing away from them at the end of the alley. Preoccupied with watering the side of a trash bin, he didn't hear Pria's quiet approach from behind, and he didn't even have a chance to turn before she cracked him across the back of the head with the knobby handle of her cane. Tunkahl stood straighter for an instant and then toppled to the side, his back smacking the ground with a muffled thump.

"Quick, search him," Pria said as she moved to crouch next to Tunkahl. "I'll get this side, you check that one."

"He's all wet now," Fairy protested.

"Just do it! We've not got all night."

Pria felt inside his right jacket pocket, but there was nothing but lint. She then shoved a hand into the man's right trouser pocket. Fairy was right. His lower half was soaked now, and Pria thought she should have chosen a more opportune time for laying him out. Too late for that now. Her hand found something in that pocket, but when she pulled it out, she saw it was a small purse full of coins. Normally a good prize, but that's not what they were looking for this time.

"Here it is," Fairy said. She was holding up a key, large and brassy in the moonlight. Fairy shook her hand in disgust after Pria took the key from her. The previous night, they'd seen Tunkahl twice. He'd come around once to the vault as the keybearer to unlock the big door, and a couple hours later he'd come back as the man in the booth pulling the lever while someone else worked the vault lock.

Out from the waist of Pria's trousers came the small, fat candle that she'd tucked in there when she'd stopped by the candlemaker's earlier. Pressed into her hip all night, the wax had softened around the edges. Pria pushed the key into the side of the candle and gave it several hard presses with her thumbs. It sank partway into the wax. Satisfied that it had left a good enough impression, she pulled the key back off the candle with care and tossed it across Tunkahl's fallen body to Fairy. "Put it back."

"Back in there?" Fairy asked, pointing to his pocket. "I only just dried my hands!"

"Put it back." Pria looked at the small purse she'd pulled out from his other pocket. "We're taking this with us."

"You're robbing him as well?"

"It's better this way. When he wakes up with a bleeding huge headache, he'll see his seri's missing, and he won't even think about that key."

Fairy wrinkled her nose as she gingerly shoved the key back into his wet pocket. "You seem experienced in this type of thing."

"Do I?" Pria gave her a wink, and she was up again, scampering back down the alley, and heard Fairy following not far behind.

# CHAPTER 8

"What do we do with the candle now?" Fairy asked, jogging to keep up with Pria. Pria's walking pace was quick, and her legs were longer, and getting the best of one of Kam Dhaz's strongarms had invigorated her.

"We get a duplicate key made," Pria said and took a sudden turn to the right that almost made Fairy stumble.

"How do we do that?"

"There." Pria pointed, and Fairy squinted in the dark.

"Locksmith," Fairy read.

Pria had seen the sign above the door several times, just a jumble of letters until now. "Right."

"Are they even open at this hour?"

Pria laughed at Fairy. "What time you think a locksmith in the East Ward would be open? Bright noonday?" She gave the front door of the business a shove and followed it inside.

The front room of the shop was small, lit by a single gaslamp hung on the wall to the right of the entrance. A short counter split the room, an assortment of metal pieces, rods, and components spread across it. Behind the counter was a doorway to the back of the shop, and Pria could see part of the workshop through it.

"Brius!" she called.

The metallic thump of something being dropped onto a wooden table answered, and then the proprietor peeked around the corner. He looked as though he'd missed a few days' worth of shaves, just like the last time she saw him. His hair was gray and unkempt, with a brown beret trying to slip off the top of his head. The man wore a stained apron and was wiping his hands on it as he leaned to see who was calling for him. When he recognized the visitor, his tiny eyes crinkled into a smile. "Pria!" When he grinned, there were more gaps than teeth showing. "What brings ye to see Brius tonight?"

"Need a key," she said and pulled the candle out from her pocket. She tossed it onto the counter, and it stuck with a thud, the impression of Tunkahl's original key facing upward.

Brius came into the front room and continued wiping grease from his hands as he studied the candle. "Suppose you need this soon, eh?"

"Tonight, if you can do it."

He laughed. "I can do it, alright. Can you pay for the trouble?"

"I can pay, you greedy dog." Pria dropped one of Tunkahl's coins on the counter. Five seri.

Brius looked at the coin and then back at Pria, an eyebrow raised now.

Pria put her hands on her hips. "Oh, for the love of —" But she stopped and stared back at Brius. "Fine." She shoved her hand back into her pocket and threw another coin onto the counter. "But I want it tonight, and I want it perfect. Compre?"

Brius' palm covered both coins and slid them off the counter into his other hand. He smiled back, with the tip of his tongue poking through the gap in his lower teeth. "Oh, aye. Brius compres."

Pria grabbed Fairy's wrist and dragged her back out the door and into the street.

"Where are we going now?" Fairy asked. There was a nervousness in her voice, and Pria wondered again how this girl had survived in the Ward without being gobbled up and spit out, much less as part of Scrounger's gang.

"To the livestock auction house. I have two—" Pria hesitated to say they were her friends, but they were, after a fashion, weren't they? "Friends," she finally said. "Lump and Cricket. They're part of Barween's gang, too. The three of us like to go there on auction days to see the animals." Pria set off down the street again, this time to the north, toward the warehouses outside the Ward, where workers shuffled goods to and from the port of Klubridge, even farther north through the enormous city.

Fairy lingered for a moment, but Pria knew she'd be along. And so she was, and it didn't take long for them to get out of the Ward and into the southeastern edge of Candlestick, just a few blocks from the port. The streets they'd been walking all night were not safe ones, and Pria thought Fairy wouldn't have lasted five minutes on her own. The eyes on these streets knew Pria, though, and their owners knew better than to accost her when she was in a hurry and swinging that cane at her side.

When they arrived at the auction house, the windows were dark, and a heavy padlock shut the barn doors at the side. "Well, we're not getting in there," Fairy said.

"Don't need to," Pria answered and beckoned her around the side, to the livestock scale that sat out next to the roadway with a sturdy awning over it. "They weigh the cows and pigs and whatnot out here."

"Were your parents farmers?"

Pria froze and shot a perplexed glance back at Fairy. "Farmers? What the hells do my parents have to do with anything?"

"I just thought that might've been why you like animals so much."

"I just like them. Let's not get carried away," she said and stepped onto the big metal square. It reminded her of the much smaller one in the booth outside Kam Dhaz's vault. "And anyway, the only farming my parents did was hunting up another hit of frost for my mum. She was an addict, and my da was a weakling."

"Oh," Fairy said, quieter. "I'm sorry. I didn't know."

"Course you didn't," Pria said. She felt the scale sink a little with her weight, but not much, given that it was intended for huge animals. Still, this scale should suffice. "You probably didn't even know your own mum or da."

"No, I didn't."

"Better that way." Pria walked to the metal rod that stood at the edge of the scale and tapped the weights until it balanced. Ninety-five, give or take. The guards all weighed one ninety-three, if Tunkahl had been telling the truth. That left—

"Ninety-eight pounds," Fairy said, leaning across to look at the weights Pria had moved. "That's the difference to make up if you're the one pulling the lever."

"If I am? I am the one," Pria said and stepped off the scale. "You're littler than me, and besides, you know what the bleeding gem looks like. You'll be the one going in the door." She didn't mention that Fairy also would be the one stuck inside if anything went wrong, and that door slammed shut.

"Still, that's more than double your weight. You'll be carrying more than you even weigh yourself. How do we make that work?"

Pria already had been trying to figure that out. She'd had no notion of her own weight until she got on that scale, but she hadn't expected that huge of a difference. She'd been expecting to go in the booth with something heavy in her pockets. Now she knew that wouldn't do the trick, not even close. "I don't know," she admitted. Not something she liked to say to anyone, much less this little rat. She sat on the curb next to the auction house and held the cane across her knees.

Fairy dropped to sit next to her. They sat in silence for a few minutes, thinking. Fairy asked, "You really think you're going to take over Klubridge?"

"The gangs, yeah. You don't think I can?"

"It's an awfully big job."

"I'll have help."

"Lump and Cricket?" Fairy asked.

"They'll be the start, sure. Then we grow it from there. Won't be long before I'm pulling recruits away from all the other gangs. Might even be a place for you," Pria said. She hadn't thought about it before speaking it, but there it was. And she didn't hate the idea of having Fairy on her side.

Fairy cut a glance at her and grinned. "Ask me again once you've at least gotten rid of Barween and Scrounger."

"That's a deal." Pria grinned back and punched her knuckles against Fairy's.

Fairy sat taller. "Oh, I have an idea!"

"Yeah? Out with it, then!"

"My friend, Dorrin—"

"The one who stole the gem."

"Right. He had an idea for trousers with pockets

that went all the way down the legs, so you could keep more in them when you, well…"

"When you went thieving," Pria said, not sure where this was going.

"Well, yes. So I made him some like that, with drawstrings that would keep everything from just piling up around his legs. He couldn't run if it did like that. The way I made it, it would spread out the weight up and down his legs."

"And you're going to make me some trousers to, what, carry a bunch of weights in?"

"I couldn't do it that fast, but we can make something similar. So you'd be wearing the extra weight instead of carrying it."

"What do you have that weighs near a hundred pounds that I can wear in some creation of yours?"

For once, Fairy was the one with a wild gleam in her eye. "You leave that to me."

# CHAPTER 9

B rius finished the key sooner than Pria had
expected, but she wasn't about to praise him for
his speed. She grabbed the newly made key off the
counter with a surly grunt of thanks, but she truly was
amazed by how much it resembled the key Fairy had
fished out of that soaked pocket. It could be that key's
twin, down to the coloring, and she hadn't even given
Brius guidance there. Still, he did take ten seri for the
job, so she reckoned it should have been an even better
job than it was.

It took Fairy less than half a day to put together the
garment she had promised Pria. When they met
outside Scrounger's den around noon, Fairy held up
her creation.

"Was this a potato sack?" Pria asked, running a hand
along the material.

"It was what I could find. It'll work," Fairy said.
"Now look. You wrap it around your waist, like so.

61

There are straps attached that go over your shoulders like this. Your suspenders gave me the idea." Fairy was securing herself into the thing as she spoke. "The part that wraps around you is like a tube, see? And at this end, there's an opening. You close that off with this drawstring." She tugged on the string, and Pria watched the hole in the end of the tube pull shut.

She was impressed but was as unlikely to congratulate Fairy for this invention as she was to praise Brius for his. "All right, so we got what I'll wear. What makes it heavy now?"

"Sand," Fairy said. "There's construction going on near Kam Dhaz's vault. I spotted it this morning, and they have more sand there than they know what to do with. They're filling in an entrance to the tunnels."

"Tunnels?"

"There are old tunnels all underneath Klubridge," Fairy said. "Scrounger's obsessed with them. He says pirates left their treasure down there or there's magic stones down there or who knows what."

"Is that true? About the pirates and all?"

Fairy shrugged. "I don't know. There are tunnels, but you'd never catch me in them. Anyway, they're blocking off one of the old entryways and building a shop or some such where it used to be."

"So, what, we scoop up a bunch of sand into the belt thing? How do we know how much to get?"

"We don't, at first. We get as much as we can cram into it, and then we go back to the auction scale and pour out the extra sand until you're the right weight."

Fairy really had figured this out. Pria had to be contrary, though. "And what about me, prancing through the streets with a hundred or more pounds of sand round my waist?"

"That's not going to be the strangest thing people see in Klubridge today. And you can drop it at the booth after we've gotten the gem."

"This whole harness thing?"

"Easy," Fairy said. She pulled up the shoulder strap on her left and showed Pria where it connected to the front of the waist belt. There was a metal clasp holding it on. "When we're finished, you just give this strap a hard tug down and then up." She did it, holding the belt steady with her other hand. The clasp let go with a click, and the belt fell away. "Just leave this behind, and you're out of it."

Pria stared at what Fairy had made. It was quite brilliant, even if she couldn't admit it aloud. She tried to find a problem and couldn't. "Looks like a solid plan," she said. "Let's do it."

Fairy gaped. "What, now?"

"No time better. It's midday, and nobody'll be there for hours. We got what we need with us." She held up the key for Fairy to see and then palmed it back into her pocket. "Let's do it. Sooner done, the better." And the sooner she'd lose Fairy somewhere in the streets of the Ward and make off with that gem.

Fairy clearly wasn't expecting to be doing this so soon, but even she had to know they were better off getting it over with. Less chance for Tunkahl to figure out he'd been had, less chance for Scrounger to find his gem missing. Pria wasn't surprised when Fairy finally nodded. "Okay, let's go get the sand."

They swapped the belt and harness over to Pria on the way to the work site Fairy had found. Once they got there, it was easy to scoop up enough sand to fill the whole compartment while the workers were off having their midday break. What wasn't easy was holding the belt harness up after it started getting full. Pria's shoulders ached with the weight of the haul, and she had to stop Fairy from shoveling more sand.

"I can't carry this," Pria said, grunting as she tried to shift the straps around.

Fairy stepped back. "You can't go halfway across the Ward like that. I think you could hold it once we get you there, though."

"You do, do you? Glad to have your confidence."

"Do you need help?" Fairy asked.

"No," Pria said with a grunt and shifted the weight on her right shoulder again. It slipped, and she nearly fell on her face.

"Yes, you do," Fairy said. "I'll unsnap the belt, and we'll carry it through the streets together. We can put it back on you when it's the right weight and we're at Dhaz's door."

And that's how they made it down the road, with each of them cradling one end of the bulky, stuffed waist pouch. Pria reminded herself the load would get lighter after they reached the livestock auction house, and so it did. Fairy kept an eye out while Pria stood on the scale, once more wearing the heavy harness, and messed with the sliders. When she began, the weights balanced out over two hundred pounds, all told. Pria carefully loosened the end of the belt and poured sand out, off to the side of the scales, before checking the weight again. She did it five times before the sliding weights at last balanced on exactly one hundred ninety-three pounds. There likely was a tolerance of a few pounds, one way or the other. That man in the tavern better have told the truth about his weight, or this whole thing would end in a disappointing fashion.

As certain as she'd sounded when she told Fairy nobody would be at the vault in the middle of the day, Pria felt her stomach aching as they neared the street with the building, lugging the sand between them. What if someone showed up while they were midway through their heist? What if someone already was inside when they opened the door?

She shook her head and pushed herself to teeter faster down the road. No use in worrying about it until there was a reason to worry about it. Let doubt creep in, and everything would go wrong. That's how she handled her jobs with Cricket and Lump, and that's how she'd handle this one with Fairy.

And the place was deserted, after all, just like she'd said. The street was quiet at this time of day, too. The East Ward got busiest after sundown, when the cutthroats were out cutting throats and the purse snatchers were snatching purses. Not much for anyone to do in the Ward in the sunlight, and not much use in them being around.

Pria fished the key out of her pocket before letting the sand-filled belt settle around her waist once more. She gave the key a toss, and Fairy caught it out of the air. Good reflexes, that.

"I wait till you're in the booth," Fairy said.

Pria nodded. "Then you turn the key in the lock. That done, I pull the lever, and we see what happens." She dearly hoped that would be the vault door opening, Fairy retrieving the gem, and the two of them escaping without incident. If anything went awry, though, Pria was more than prepared to drop the sand and leg it out of there, Fairy be damned. She looked for a long moment at the other girl and swallowed. She could abandon her, sure. No reason to fret over it, and Pria would find some other treasure some other day. No remorse. Sure.

"You ready?" Fairy asked, concern creasing between her eyes. She'd seen something in Pria's face.

"Never readier." Pria paused outside the booth when she realized the belt made her hips wider than the doorway. She tilted the harness a little and wedged herself through at an angle. Her legs wobbled under the weight, and Pria finally popped free and was in the booth, standing on the metal plate. She felt it sink beneath her feet, just like the scales had done at the auction house.

She looked out through the door at Fairy and nodded. Fairy nodded back and slid the key into the big lock. For a wild instant, Pria was afraid the key Brius had given her wouldn't work. Of course, it did work, and she heard the first locking mechanism clank open as Fairy gave it a twist.

Now it was her turn. Pria grasped the lever in front of her and gave it a pull. It slid smoothly toward her, rotating slow and sure in its housing. They'd gotten the weight right, and Fairy's harness contraption had worked. This really was working!

When the lever reached its lowest point, it gave a jolt, and Pria nearly lost her grip on it. She held on, though, and that was when she realized the lever wanted to slide back up to its original position. She would have to hold the handle down the entire time the door was open. And open, the door did. It gave a thud, the same sound she and Fairy had heard every time Dhaz's minions had opened it, and now it swung outward.

Fairy held the edge of the door and pulled it the rest of the way open. She peered into the doorway, and Pria desperately wanted to know what she was seeing. All that time spent on the roof watching this place, and she'd never seen what was inside and never would. Unfair, but this was how it had to go. Fairy gave Pria one last glance before she stepped through the entrance and disappeared into the building.

The longer Pria held the lever, the heavier the sand felt. And the heavier the sand felt, the more her hand sweated on that lever. She wondered if she might be able to just drop the belt on the floor. It would still be the same weight on the plate as before, but she just wouldn't have to hold it up. Should've thought of that before. Now she couldn't let go of the lever, and she couldn't get the shoulder strap off over her right hand in that position. She just had to wait and keep holding it.

What was taking Fairy so long? Was she in trouble? Or had she found the gem, located some back exit from the place, and left Pria literally holding the bag? Surely she wouldn't have done that. Fairy was the trusting one. The one who didn't know the streets the way Pria did. Pria's the one who would steal that gem and abandon her partner, not the other way around. Right? Pria cursed. She couldn't even go and look in the door to see what was going on. As soon as she let go of the lever, the door would slam shut, likely trapping Fairy inside.

Pria didn't know how long she'd been waiting, but it felt like forever by the time Fairy at last emerged. Pria lurched in surprise but kept her fingers on the lever. Fairy held up something in her hand. Something green. It had to be the gem. Now Fairy was moving past the booth. Was she planning to run off with it, after all? That's why she'd been so agreeable to weigh Pria down in the booth, wasn't it?

Pria snarled and released the lever. It chunked back into place, and the vault door outside the booth swung shut. Pria lurched off the metal plate, but her still-bulging belt bounced her off the doorway, and only then did she think to yank on the left strap. The belt dropped away and hit the floor, the sand spilling out across the plate and onto the rough wood surrounding it. As soon as it landed, something clanked in the booth's wall to Pria's right. She spun to see what it was, and behind her a metal door slid in from the right, sealing the booth.

What was this? They had seen nothing like that door in all the time they'd watched this place.

Of course they hadn't. This was a security mechanism. Everybody coming and going had known how to avoid it. She and Fairy had missed something, done something wrong. Pria pushed the door and tried to slide it back into its housing, but it stood firm. No getting out that way. She clambered onto the shelf where the lever was mounted and pressed against the window above it. It looked like glass but didn't shatter when she beat and banged on it.

Fairy was just outside that window now, staring in. She was saying something, but no sound penetrated the booth. Pria slapped at her ears and yelled, "I can't hear you!" But, naturally, Fairy couldn't hear her, either.

Fairy stood there for another moment and looked down at the gem in her hand. Then back up at Pria, and then back at the gem. She mouthed something to Pria. What... It looked like she said something about hells. See you in hells? Burn in hells? Whatever it was, Pria got the message when Fairy gave her a wink, pocketed the gem, and sprinted away from the booth as fast as her legs would carry her.

"No!" Pria wailed and slapped at the glass. But it was too late. Pria knew she'd been had. That was the last she'd see of either the girl or the prize, and she was left to deal with the consequences.

That's when the booth made another grinding noise, and green fumes spewed into it around Pria's feet.

# CHAPTER 10

P ria smelled something like blood, but not quite blood. Metallic, more like. She sniffed and shifted, and that's when she realized all at once that her eyes were closed, and she didn't remember having closed them. She blinked awake and hacked out a series of rough coughs, all of them tasting like copper.

"You gassed me," she said once she was done with the coughing.

The man sitting across from her propped his right elbow on the arm of the chair and pressed his index finger into his temple and his thumb along a severe jawline. His black hair was long and pulled back from his clean-shaven face. "Do you know who I am?"

Pria blinked, and her eyes were sticky. She tried to wipe at them but found that her hands were tied to the arms of her own chair. She remembered Therron Bel all tied up and thrown over Lump's shoulder and gave a quick laugh before she thought about how Bel was probably dead now. "You're Kam Dhaz."

"How do you know who I am?" He frowned at her and uncrossed his legs and then crossed them over the other way.

"Your fancy gray suit, for one. And I'd wager that gold bracelet's worth a pretty penny. Everybody knows you're the money in the Ward. Oh, and there's the matter of you finding me in your bleeding rat trap or whatever the hells that thing is."

It was a guess, but she knew she was right. Kam Dhaz studied her for a long moment before he asked, "Who do you work for?"

Pria tried her feet, but cords bound her ankles to the legs of the chair, just as she suspected. No getting up anytime soon. She craned her neck and looked around the room where Dhaz was holding her. All three walls she could see were painted yellow, and there were lamps with flickering flames mounted on all of them. Shelves lined those walls, and there were tables below the shelves. All sorts of objects and oddities lined nearly every square inch of space. Pria saw clocks, baskets, musical instruments. It was a bizarre assortment, and Pria knew she had to be inside the vault.

Dhaz put two fingers on Pria's chin and pulled her attention back to his face. "Who do you work for?"

"What is all this stuff?" she asked and jerked her head at one of the walls.

Dhaz sat back, still looking at her. Then he stood,

the fabric of his tailored pants uncreasing and falling precisely to just above his shiny black shoes. Dhaz's gaze moved away from Pria as he stepped to her right and picked up a thick gilded rod, about two feet long. It flared out on one end, where an arrangement of tiny, thin strips of gold topped it, forming into a box-shaped ornament. "This," Dhaz said, holding the cylindrical part of the rod in one hand and carefully resting the decorative top in the other, "is Vhodresh's scepter." His thin lips pulled into what Pria thought he intended to be a smile but looked more like a gaka worm. When he saw that no recognition had registered on her face, he said it again. "Vhodresh's scepter."

Pria tried to shrug, but the ropes made it weaker than she'd intended. "Sorry, no idea."

"You surely know who Vhodresh was," he said. His voice was insistent, and he was leaning forward now, his eyes intense.

Pria bit at her cheek and made a show of thinking. She'd landed on something Dhaz was interested in. If she could keep him talking, she might learn more about what he intended for her. And the longer he talked, the longer she'd live if, as was likely, he intended to kill her and dump her in an alley. "Sorry." She shook her head. "No idea."

He scowled at her. "Vhodresh was the governor of Aramore more than two centuries ago. Surely you know of Aramore?"

"Stuffy place to the north? Probably cold there," she said. Of course she bloody knew what Aramore was.

"After Vhodresh was deposed, the new governor had him executed. His scepter fell into the black market and seemed lost. I acquired it nearly five years ago, and it has resided here since then." He placed the rod back in its space on the shelf with a carefulness that was not lost on Pria. He really cared about this junk. This was what was important to him. This was what all his underhanded efforts in Klubridge worked towards. He was nothing more than a collector.

"How bout that one?" Pria asked and rocked her head to the left. Dhaz crossed the room to the shelves on the opposite side.

"This?" he asked and touched the edge of a small picture frame.

"No, next to it."

He pointed to a book lying on its edge with lettering on the spine that Pria couldn't read.

"No, the other way."

He sighed and picked up a bowl that looked like it was earthen and old. "The Minine Bowl," he said, as if that should mean anything. Maybe it would have if Pria had taken any kind of interest in historical nonsense, but she knew the here and now was more important if you wanted to survive and thrive in the East Ward.

"What dead man did that belong to, then?" she asked.

The corner of his mouth turned up in a smirk. "Many. The Minine Bowl is cursed."

"It's ugly enough to be."

He ignored her insult and launched into his explanation. "For generations, this bowl has brought misfortune to its owners. The person who takes ownership of the bowl inevitably falls into chaos, failure, and usually death."

"Should we be expecting you to knock over anytime now?" Pria asked. "Seeing as you own that ugly thing?"

"Ah," he said, "but I am not the owner. One of my associates gained this piece from its previous owner and brought it here. He placed it in this very room for safekeeping. My associate was the owner of this bowl. I merely oversee its safekeeping."

"Was? Meaning you topped him after he got your knickknack for you. In which case, seems to me like you're the owner now."

"No." He was frowning again. "This bowl has no owner."

Pria raised the corner of her mouth in doubt. "Not how it seems to me. I say you're splitting hairs, and you own that thing. You're basically doomed, way I see it."

Dhaz looked at the bowl cupped in his hands and then at Pria. "What if I gift it to you, eh? How would you like to take possession of the Minine Bowl yourself?"

"So you do own it, then. You can't very well give me something's not yours, compre?"

Dhaz bared his clenched teeth at Pria. He sat the bowl back in its place and turned to face her again, a finger in her face. "You mock an enchanted artifact, girl. You mock magic itself."

"No such thing," she said, and she meant it. All the

talk about magic, and she'd seen nothing to convince her it was real.

His eyebrows went up. "You don't believe in magic," he said, and it was more a puzzled statement than a question.

"Nope. Way I see it, the Empire likes to wave that around to scare everybody into doing what they want, yeah? Probably ain't even a real High Lord. He's just another thing they made up. You ever seen magic?"

"Of course I have!" He was incredulous. "Everyone has seen magic done at one time or another."

"Not in the East Ward. Not in my life," she said and snorted. Some residue from the gas was still in her nose. Pria remembered the green vapor that had spewed into the booth from a hidden hatch somewhere along the floor. She sniffed once more and turned her head to spit a green glob onto the ground.

Dhaz stared at the mess like he'd never seen such in his life. Then he was back to Pria. "Who do you work for?"

"Who do you work for?" she asked back at him. "That locking contraption, the weight thing in the floor, the lever, the gas. All that's got to be Imperial engineering. How'd you come by it?"

He clenched his jaw, and she saw the pulse in his temple. She'd gotten to him with that one. But then he regained his composure. "The Gem of Tagath is missing. I know someone was with you and took it, and you're going to tell me who and where I can find them to get it back."

"Can't do, Kam." If she thought giving up Fairy would earn her freedom, she'd have done it in an instant. But she knew she had to hold that information back. It probably was the only thing keeping her alive. "Why did you have them make the locks like that, anyway? Pretty complicated to get into, even if I hadn't been breaking in."

"I do not trust easily," he said. "I enjoy having effective security measures to protect my property. It appears that is not without need."

Pria tilted her head. "Eh, I nearly got away with it." And it was true. She would have, if she hadn't tried to get after Fairy so fast. As it was, she had doomed herself and let Fairy swipe the gem right out from under her nose. "You think that gem is magic, too, don't you? You believe the stories."

"I know it is," he said.

"People say it reveals magic. Whatever that means." Anything to keep him talking.

"It compels mages who come near the gem to reveal their magic. It's a tool the Empire has used for hundreds of years to identify and catch hidden mages at court. And you still do not even believe magic exists."

Pria tried again to shrug. "Just doesn't mean nothing to me."

"Why did you want to steal it, then? What was your purpose here?"

"Seemed like a laugh," she said and gave a mean grin.

Kam Dhaz lingered in front of her but finally pulled

his eyes away from hers. "You'll tell me what you know. Who you did this for. I may have some leniency, or I may not. Your best chance is to talk, girl." With that, he moved past her, toward the area behind her that she couldn't see. She heard something mechanical moving. That had to be the door. It slammed shut, and the wall lamps flickered out into darkness all at the same time. Pria sat alone in that darkened vault, unable to move and unable to see.

"You've done it now," she whispered and saw Fairy again in her mind's eye. The girl wasn't running, wasn't trying to pull anything. Not until Pria lunged at her and set off the trap. No, they would have gotten away together if Pria had been calm and trusted her. She grunted and hated thinking Barween had been even a little bit right. If she had trusted that girl, she wouldn't be in this situation. But instead, here she was, tied to a chair and likely to die in the middle of a room full of old junk.

# CHAPTER 11

At some point, Pria must have fallen asleep or, more likely, passed out again from the remnants of the gas she'd inhaled. She didn't know when she'd drifted off or for how long, but she woke with a start when the door behind her made the familiar clang of unlocking.

As the door slid open, the flames leaped to life in the lamps on the walls, lit automatically by some hidden mechanisms. Pria looked around the room, frantic, and tried her arms and legs again. The ropes still bound them to the chair, of course, and now she could feel the pins and needles in them from the bindings being too tight.

Was this it? Was this when they'd come back to kill her?

The sound of footsteps came into the room with her, and then an arm appeared from her right, a blade gleaming in the hand. This was it, then. They were cutting her throat and making done with her.

Only, it wasn't. The knife sliced through the cord at her right wrist, and the whole thing went slack all over. They were freeing her!

Pria yanked her right arm loose and grabbed at the loops around her left while she shuffled her feet around. Her fingers were numb and white, but she extracted herself from the chair, and she stumbled forward, turning as she went.

Kam Dhaz was folding the knife into itself, the blade some sort of mechanical curiosity. It slid into his sleeve before Pria could see how it worked. But then something even more bizarre than the knife pulled her attention past Dhaz and to the doorway leading outside.

"Fairy?" she asked. What was happening? Did Fairy work for Kam Dhaz all along? Was this all an elaborate scam? No, Fairy looked terrified. And almost as terrified as Fairy, here came Lump and Cricket behind her, their faces wary and bewildered. Lump had only just finished stepping through the door when it hissed and slid shut behind him. The lock slammed back into place inside the wall.

"What is this?" Pria asked, this time to Dhaz.

"You have some loyal friends," Dhaz said and gestured to Fairy. "This one has come to bargain for your life."

Pria's eyes moved between Dhaz and Fairy. This

made no sense. "You left me!" she said. "You ditched me. What are you doing back here?"

Fairy's face showed hurt. "I'd never! I told you I was going to get help!"

Go to hells. Going to get help. A simple mistake to make, apparently. Pria would have laughed if she were not still so confused. "How are you going to bargain for my life? And what are you two doing here?"

Cricket shrugged. "This one came and got us, said you was in a bad way."

"And so we all meet merrily," Kam Dhaz said, an annoyed tone moving into his voice. "You have seen that she is alive. I believe you have something for me," he said to Fairy.

She slipped a hand into her trouser pocket, and it came out closed over something. Pria knew what it was going to be before the girl turned her fist over and opened her fingers. The bleeding Gem of bloody Tagath. Dhaz plucked it from her palm and carried it to the shelves on the left of the room, midway between where Fairy stood and where Pria was trying to balance herself with a hand on a railing, next to where Dhaz had put his stupid scepter thing.

Whatever that gas had been, it still played with her balance, but most of her coordination was coming back. Still, she would have sworn she was hallucinating. Why was this gutter rat giving up one of the Imperial gems to save Pria, a girl she hardly knew? Wasn't getting that gem the whole point of their meeting in the first place?

"Now we go," Fairy said.

As he placed the gem back on a small pillow where it likely had been resting before Fairy stole it, Dhaz's mouth drew into that thin smile again. Pria knew it would not be that simple.

"Do you know what this is?" Dhaz asked and lifted a wickedly sharp sword off a short platform next to where he'd displayed the gem. The sword's hilt was brass, with black cords woven into it. The blade itself was silver and shiny, almost straight but with a slight curve to it, nearly two feet long. Although the tip was blunt, probably worn down in battle, the rest of the blade would do the job plenty well.

Dhaz turned the sword and sliced it through the air as he stepped closer to Fairy. Cricket took a step back, placing Fairy between himself and the sword. Lump tried to step backwards, too, but he was already up against the wall with the closed door in it.

"This is called a katana," Dhaz said. "This particular katana has been known by several names throughout history. Eclipse, one of its owners called it. To another, it was the Time Defiler. Do you know why they called it that?"

"Your sword has the same problem as your stories," Pria said.

Dhaz angled his head, annoyed at being interrupted, and half turned. "No point to any of them," she finished and swung the scepter of whatever it was called directly at his face.

She'd swung it hard and true, just like swinging her

cane. The delicate gold froppery at the end of the thing exploded when it collided with Kam Dhaz's head, and Pria felt the satisfying thunk vibrate all the way up the rod and into her arms. Dhaz's head smacked back against the shelf behind him, and the man crumpled to the ground without another word. The sword of doomy whatsit bounced out of his hand and skittered harmlessly under a low bench a few feet away.

"You've killed him!" Fairy shrieked, and at the same instant, Lump cheered.

Pria tossed the scepter away and shushed them. "There's a guard outside working the lever in the booth, yeah? Where's our key to this door?"

Fairy winced. "I lost it. I was in such a hurry to get to Barween's and find these two. Would a key even work from the inside?"

"Has to," Pria said and pointed to Dhaz on the floor. "He wouldn't be in here with the door shut if it wouldn't. We've just got to take this sod's key and get out and leg it before whoever's out there can get after us. Won't help if they hear us first."

Fairy nodded and dropped to her knees beside Dhaz's still body. She already had her hands going through his pockets. "He's not dead," she said, and she sounded relieved.

"Why did you come back for me, squeak?"

Fairy looked up from her search. "You'd have done the same for me." And then she was back at it again, her hand down the side pocket on Dhaz's suit trousers.

Pria watched the girl at work and swallowed hard.

Lump and Cricket were watching her, looking for directions. Her breath hitched, and she forced herself into motion. She knelt across from Fairy and started searching Dhaz's pockets on the opposite side. But Fairy already had it. "Here's the key," she said and held it up, just like she'd done with the identical pee-soaked key she'd dug out of Tunkahl's pocket in that grimy alley.

"Well done," Pria muttered. She slid the gold bracelet off Dhaz's wrist before she pushed herself up from the floor. She took the key from Fairy and stepped over the unconscious body. Her hat and cane sat discarded on the floor to the right of the entrance. Pria grabbed both and turned to the door as she settled the hat back onto her head where it belonged.

"Wait," Fairy said, and Pria paused. "I need this." Fairy scooped the Gem of Tagath off the pillow where Dhaz had placed it, and she dropped it into her pocket where it had been when she arrived at the vault just a few minutes ago. Of course she needed it. How had Pria forgotten to swipe that bloody thing herself? Too much going on all at once.

"Good now?" Pria asked and rested her hand on Fairy's elbow.

"Dice," Fairy said and smiled at her. It was a nervous smile, but it was genuine, and it made Pria's chest ache.

"Let's go, then." Pria shooed Lump away from the door and held the key in front of the lock. "Don't forget, we're running as soon as we get out. Split up, make it harder to get chased."

Cricket nodded, but Lump drew his brows together. "Be easier with better shoes."

Fairy grabbed Pria's hand and squeezed it. "Thank you, Pria. For helping with the gem. For everything."

Pria glanced at her and turned the key. The door slid open, and Pria shoved it the rest of the way. Somebody had to be continuing to hold that lever outside.

Lump and Cricket were out first, running straight ahead together and disappearing around the corner without splitting up. Fairy was next, no doubt headed straight to Scrounger's place to slip the gem back into wherever he'd been keeping it. Pria was last and paused. In the instant before going through the door, she looked into her hand, where she'd palmed the gem right out of the other girl's pocket.

"Sorry, Fairy," she whispered, and she ran.

# CHAPTER 12

There had indeed been a guard outside, and as she blew past the booth, Pria recognized the stocky woman she'd seen there while on reconnaissance. The woman's mouth opened and closed, and her eyes were big and round as she watched the four kids blast out the door of the vault and scatter.

Pria didn't know which one of them the guard had followed, if she'd even followed any of them. Pria's eyes were on the road ahead, and she had one hand holding her cane tucked up under her arm and the other pressed on the pocket where she'd deposited the gem. Couldn't let that thing go toppling out after all this. The effects of the gas thankfully had run their course, and Pria was able to pump her legs as hard and fast as ever.

The wind nearly took her hat a couple of times, but it stayed on her head all the way through her crazed flight across the Ward. She stayed off the major roads, so there wasn't much traffic, and the people she encountered scrambled out of the way of the demonic girl tearing up the roadway.

Pria didn't stop running until she reached a cross street at least ten blocks from where she had left Dhaz's hideout. She was breathing hard by then, and there was the hint of a cramp in her side, so she held onto the brick corner of an old apartment house and peered back in the direction she'd come. Nobody was after her. That guard couldn't have kept up with her even if she'd tried, but Pria would wager that woman had gone straight to the door to try and figure a way into the vault to see what had become of her boss, rather than worrying about a bunch of gutter mongrels on the run.

Once she'd recovered and no longer was panting for air, Pria wiped her hand across her forehead and pushed a strand of sweaty hair up under her hat. With the other hand, she dug the gem out of her pocket. Being careful not to show it off for every passerby to see, Pria cupped the jewel and stared at it. It was only a couple of inches across the top, but Pria figured that was plenty huge for such a thing. She'd never seen a real gem in person before this one, so her reckoning might have been off.

It was green, sure enough, and the sun pushed through it to leave a leaf-colored stain on Pria's skin. She rolled the gem around and watched the colored light patterns play through it and change the shape of the projection on her palm.

This was it, alright. One of the Imperial gems, and it was right here in her hand. People believed all that magic nonsense about it, whatever Kam Dhaz had been going on about. Pria didn't believe in magic, not one lick. But it was fine with her if other people believed in it and feared it, especially when she could hold something like the Gem of Tagath over them.

This would legitimize her. Nobody would question why she'd be running her own gang if they knew she controlled an Imperial gem. She'd have to be careful not to let the City Watch catch her with it, naturally, but this could work. She could collect Cricket and Lump, and that would be the start of it. No more Barween, no more running jobs for other people. She'd be calling the shots, and it would be all because she had this gem and could make people respect her.

Fairy.

The thought came unbidden, just like the other girl had shown up unexpectedly to rescue Pria from Dhaz. As soft as she was about everything, Fairy ought've been run down in the street already. She wouldn't make it in the East Ward. It didn't matter whether she took that gem back to Scrounger. She'd catch a beating from somebody, somewhere, one way or another. She believed having that gem back would save her a threshing.

Pria closed her hand over the gem again and cursed.

She peeked at it one more time before dropping it back into her pocket and taking the street to the left, not toward Barween's where she could find her own crew, but down into the muck. Down toward Scrounger's hovel.

# CHAPTER 13

It didn't take Pria long to find Scrounger's place again, slouched on the corner of that run-down street. Her stride faltered for a second when she saw Fairy standing outside the door. She was frantic, rubbing at her pockets and feeling anywhere she might have stowed the gem and forgotten about it. Then her eyes met Pria's, and she knew.

"You!" Fairy yelled and stomped off the curb and into the street to meet her. "You took it from me!"

Pria held up a hand. "Shush. Is Scrounger inside?"

Fairy stopped and blinked at her but then began her attack anew. Pria couldn't blame her. "I trusted you!"

"That was your mistake," Pria snapped back. "Now tell me, is Scrounger inside or isn't he?"

Fairy's eyes brimmed with tears, and Pria couldn't look at that for another instant. She sidestepped the younger girl and pushed her way through the door and into Scrounger's den. It was midday, and all his little cretins were asleep in the front room, piled here and there on dirty rags or soft spots where the wooden floor was rotting away. It was a sad affair, worse than anything she'd seen at Barween's, but that wasn't why Pria had come.

A head raised up from a filthy pile of blankets in the corner, and Pria recognized the swollen and bruised face. "Oy, Skink. Where's Scrounger?"

The boy squinted at her in the dark of the room and pointed toward the back, where another ragged piece of burlap hung over a doorway that led deeper into the shack. Pria pulled it aside and ducked underneath. She was in a small room, little more than a hallway, with a door leading out the back and a rickety staircase going down in front of her. The flicker of lamplight crawled up from the basement, and she followed it down.

Pria ducked as she headed down the stairs, and the underground room came into view. It was an office of sorts. Old wood paneling on the walls, a desk toward the center, warped file cabinets against the back wall. And there, behind the desk, was the man she'd come to see. He sat hunched over some papers, his shoulders rounded, the bald spot showing at the top of his head. Scraggly dark hair surrounded it and poured down onto his face in a thick and unruly beard.

The next-to-last step creaked under Pria's foot, and Scrounger's head came up. He stared at her with wet, beady eyes. "Who are you?" he asked with a rumble Pria could feel in her chest. His casualness nearly threw her off her swagger, but the swagger was important.

Her confidence was all she had for this meeting, so she pressed forward.

"My name's Pria," she said. There was no second chair, so she perched on the corner of the desk, half turned to face the man. She thought he looked more like a bear than a man, even though she'd only seen bears in drawings. "You'd know me soon enough anyway, but I wanted to be courteous and introduce myself."

He clasped his hands on the desk and sat back in his chair. The wood creaked with his weight, and he stared at her from beneath bushy black eyebrows.

"I've taken a problem off your hands."

His eyebrows twitched for a brief instant. "You have, have you?"

"I heard you recently came into possession of something that's like to be nothing but trouble for you. Not something you'd be able to sell. Not something you could brag about or show off."

"And where might you have heard that, pray?"

"Here and there," Pria said. "The important thing is, you don't got to worry about it anymore. I've taken it off your hands."

Scrounger's eyes never left hers, but he pushed back from the desk and heaved himself to his feet. Still watching Pria, he rounded the desk and came to the wall on the left side of the room. He rapped his thick knuckles against the wood, and a panel swung open. "You may wonder why I am opening my safe so freely with you in the room," he said. "If you've taken something from me, then you evidently already know the location of my safe, in which case I shall kill you. If you are lying to me, I shall kill you. Neither scenario ends with you leaving this room to share your knowledge."

Pria knew she was fast, and she guessed he was slow enough that she could evade his grasp and get back up those stairs before he could do anything to her, but she hoped she wouldn't have to find out.

Scrounger's gaze broke from hers long enough for him to glance into the safe, and then his eyes were back on hers, and he was advancing on her now, his hands balled into fists at his sides. "Where is it?" he barked. "What did you do with it?"

Pria forced herself not to move from the edge of the desk. He had to see that she wasn't afraid of him. Or she had to make him believe that, at least. Inside, her heart was thump-thumping like it had been after she ran away from the vault just a while ago. "I got it somewhere safe. But peace, friend. I'm not stealing from you. I'm here to trade."

He loomed over Pria, and she felt the breath from his nostrils, hot and angry. There was no getting away from him now. He was too close, and he could snap her neck if he took a notion to it. Why was she putting herself in this situation?

Fairy, she told herself, and exhaled.

"Do you know what this is?" she asked and sincerely hoped he didn't. She pulled the Minine Bowl out from where she'd stowed it in her side pocket. It had survived the sprint through the city, and she'd intended to sell it, along with that bracelet she'd lifted off Dhaz. But, standing at that cross street, she'd known what she had to do.

Scrounger glared at her, and then at the object in her hand. "It's a bowl. What of it?"

"It's not just any bowl," she said. "This came from the tunnels underneath the city. I've heard you have an interest there." She was betting everything on Fairy having been right about that.

His eyes narrowed, and he huffed out a breath. "Where did you hear that?"

"Here and there," she said again. "This bowl was in the cargo of some of the first pirates to use the tunnels. It's said to be enchanted."

"Enchanted," he said with derision, but Pria saw the interest in his tiny, dark eyes. She knew she had him on the hook. Now, if she could keep him there.

"It's connected to the rest of their loot with magic. You take this with you, and it'll lead you straight through the tunnels to where they stowed their booty." She turned the bowl in her hand and rotated it so he could see all around it. "Something like that could interest you?"

He was staring at the bowl then, and his fat tongue licked across his lips once, quickly. "You think this bowl would be worth enough to me to equal one of the Imperial gems, girl? How do I even know you're telling the truth?"

"You don't," she said. "But the gem isn't here." She thought she could feel its weight in her pocket, but surely that was just her imagination. She prayed to gods she didn't believe in that this freak wouldn't search her. "You couldn't do anything with it, anyway, even if you had it. So either you take this bowl or you don't. Either way, you're not getting the gem back today."

"I could crush your skull and keep the bowl," Scrounger said, and she knew he meant it.

"Or you could take this bowl, shove it sideways up your arse, and hope you see me to deal again someday."

His eyes pushed into hers, and she could feel the weight of the moment. This was when she either would earn some ounce of respect from this beast, or he'd demolish her, and she'd never be seen again. But, as brutal as she knew Scrounger was, she also knew he was no fool. He had no chance to recover the gem if he killed her here and now. If he let her go, he'd have another opportunity to do her in later on, when he could take a swipe at getting the gem back as well.

Even as Pria thought it, she saw the same consideration on Scrounger's face. He grunted, and she knew she'd be walking out of that basement alive.

"Give me the damned bowl," he said. Pria suppressed a laugh at the irony of his wording.

She didn't believe in that foolish curse or magic or any of the rest of it, but she still felt some satisfaction when she handed the Minine Bowl over into Scrounger's enormous hand. "It's yours," she said. "You're the new owner." If there really was such a thing as a curse, she hoped it would eat him right up.

"Now go." He pointed to the stairs. "Don't come here again."

Pria hopped off the desk and pushed the brim of her hat up with the top of her cane. "See you around." And she was gone and up the stairs.

# CHAPTER 14

"So where did you put the gem?" Fairy asked. They were sitting in an alley not far from Scrounger's den, but far enough that Pria felt safe talking.

"Nowhere," Pria said and dug into her pocket. She opened her hand and showed the gem to Fairy. It glimmered in the sunlight and cast green shapes up onto their faces.

"You had it on you the whole time you were talking to Scrounger? What if he'd checked you for it?"

"I just hoped he wouldn't, and he didn't."

Fairy gaped at Pria, and then a tentative smile played at the corners of her mouth. "He doesn't know Skink took it?"

"Nope. Wooly bastard thinks I snuck in and swiped it. No beatings for you." Pria held the gem up and closed one eye so she could look at the sun through the green, glassy prism.

"Thank you," Fairy said. "You didn't have to do that."

"No, I didn't. Don't properly know why I did." She closed her hand back around the gem again and put it in her lap.

Fairy gave her a true smile. "I do. It's because you decided you like me. We're friends."

Pria raised an eyebrow at her but couldn't keep herself from laughing. "You got me all figured out?"

"Mostly. What are you going to do with that thing, anyway?"

"Thought I might stick it on the top of my cane. What do you think?" Pria held the gem against the handle. It was just the right size.

"I think you'll get picked up by the City Watch within a day, if you go waving it about like that."

"Nah. They'll forget about it inside a week. Two at most."

"They will not, and that's a fact. That's one of the Imperial gems!" Fairy's voice lowered on the last words, as if anybody were close enough to hear.

"The Empire might care. The City Watch won't. Far as they're concerned, they already hung somebody up for it. They've got other things to worry about. This beauty is lost to time, far as Klubridge is concerned."

"Aren't you afraid Scrounger will come after you? Or somebody else will try to take it?"

"I'm not afraid of Scrounger," Pria said, and she made it sound like she believed it. "Anybody else? Who'd think I'd be stupid enough to go waving around the Gem of bleeding Tagath on the end of my cane? Looks like a fake to most. A paste jewel."

Fairy frowned. "What's the point, then?"

"The point is that not everybody'll think it's a fake. The right people will know the gem disappeared going through Klubridge, and they'll know I'm the one who's got it. People are afraid of this thing, and that makes them afraid of me."

Fairy started, "People like—"

"People like Barween bloody Drach, that's who. And Kam Dhaz and any of the others that want to question me."

"This is it, then? This is how you start your own gang?"

"It is." Pria tilted her head back and leaned it against the wall. "And then I take the East Ward. And then all of Klubridge."

"How are you going to do all that? You don't even believe that thing is magic, do you?"

Pria smiled at Fairy. "That's for tomorrow. Today's the start." She pushed herself up from the ground with her cane. "Sure you don't want a job, squeak?"

Fairy looked back up at her, and Pria knew she was thinking about it, but she wouldn't go for it. Sure enough, Fairy shook her head. "I can't. I have people here."

"Not that Skink boy."

"Not Skink. But there are other people who need me."

Pria nodded like she understood. And, in a way, she guessed she did. Cricket and Lump couldn't find their way to the privy without her guiding them. They'd be her first followers, and she guessed she'd have to learn to trust them if she had any hope of growing this thing she was about to build. "Guess that's it, then."

Fairy stood up and brushed the dirt off her rear. "That's it? You're done with me now, and we go our separate ways?"

Pria reached her finger out and poked Fairy on the nose. "You're not shed of me that easy. We'll see each other again, I'm positive. I just have things to do between now and then."

"Like what?"

Pria held the top of the cane to her chin and thought. Really thought. This was the first time she'd been able to make a big move since she'd run off from home all those years ago. She had a gang to build. She had to pry herself away from Barween. Where to begin?

"For starters," she said, "I think it's time I found Lump some decent shoes."

# CONTINUE THE ADVENTURE

*The Gem of Tagath* takes place several months prior to the first full novel in the Teshovar series. In *Akithar's Greatest Trick*, you will learn more about the gangs of Klubridge and meet the most famous stage magician in Teshovar, a realm where real magic is outlawed.

Keep reading for a look at the first scene from *Akithar's Greatest Trick*!

# AKITHAR'S GREATEST TRICK: CHAPTER 1

Sometimes, when he perched on the edge of a rooftop on a clear night like this one and looked down at the streets, Dorrin felt like a bird. He felt like he could fall forward into the night and leave the rough shingles and glide over the city, his toes brushing chimneys and his fingers cutting through the chill air. He'd ride the wind over the workers, past the stalls, beyond the guards, and above the city walls. He'd leave Klubridge behind and soar into the black sky beyond.

If Dorrin were a bird, though, he wouldn't be the kind that would simply take wing and fly away. He'd be something small, something to match his human form, which already was short and thin for an eleven-year-old. Dorrin would be quick, maybe a hummingbird, darting here and there and slipping through tiny spaces, pausing just long enough to take what nectar he could gather before speeding to the next flower.

But no, the hummingbird wasn't cunning. Dorrin

was clever. Dorrin would be a more predatory bird, watching the ground below him and preparing to dive when his eye caught the movement of prey. Even now, Dorrin's own eyes flicked quickly among the crowd, moving from the baker leaving his shop for the night to the old man leaning on a cane to the young woman carrying a bundle of what looked like potatoes. In his mind, lines connected them, visible like a golden thread glowing only for him.

He blinked twice and then let himself slip down from the roof. Instead of leaping into the air, he shimmied off the edge and dropped to the first window ledge below. From there he hopped down and caught himself on a round drainpipe and rode that the rest of the way to the street level. He'd been sitting only three stories above the road, but even that was far enough to muffle the sounds and dim the lights of one of Klubridge's major thoroughfares in the full bustle of early evening.

Up there, it was easy to see the carts and the people. They all were moving and jostling through the road to and from the shops, but with a pattern and direction that made sense. Down here, it was chaotic, and Dorrin came barely to shoulder height on most of the crowd. He was eye level with waistcoats and bundles, cloaks and bodices. He didn't need to see better than that, though. He knew where he was going. He still had that golden thread in his mind, and he sensed it pulling him out into the road.

Dorrin scampered out of the way of a horseman

and sidestepped a couple deep in an argument. None of them even noticed the boy in dirty clothes. Even if they had seen him, they likely would have looked right past him, like most of the city did with kids like him. Street kids. That served his purpose well. As he skipped between another pair, he caught sight of the baker, just a flash of white linen in the crowd. Dorrin had guessed his direction correctly, and he picked up a brisk pace to close the distance without running. The people would ignore fast walking, but running always invited trouble.

The baker was less than five steps ahead now and was making a slow pace down the street, caught behind a cart pulled by a tired donkey. Dorrin studied the situation with the speed of experience and spotted the lump low on the baker's back, just under his tunic and above his waist. The tiny sliver of sharp metal was between Dorrin's fingers by the time he was two steps behind the baker, and it sliced a precise slit in his white tunic even as Dorrin pulled alongside the man. Dorrin stayed alert, his head turning to scan the crowd as he felt the satisfying weight of the purse drop out through the cut in the fabric and into his palm.

Dorrin changed direction and slipped the bag into a deep pocket sewn into his loose trousers less than a second after he made the grab. He didn't check whether the baker had detected the change in weight around his waist. Sometimes they noticed, but by the time they did he always was long gone, either high above them on the roofs or already half a block away, too low in the crowd for them to spot him. This time he was ahead and to the right, just turning the corner as the golden thread in his mind pulled him onward.

The old man was closer than Dorrin had expected. He must have paused at a stall, or something had blocked him. No matter, it was too late to skip him. Dorrin made fast work of his appraisal and saw the leather pouch hanging from the belt around the man's waist. Dorrin matched his pace, just behind and to the left. When the man took a step and leaned to the right on his cane, Dorrin's hand slipped just past his left hip, snipping the belt cord and dropping the pouch directly into another pocket hidden in the folds of Dorrin's pants.

The boy pivoted on his left foot and angled into the flow of traffic before the old man had even completed his step. Dorrin tugged on a hidden lace to tighten the pocket, and the leather pouch bumped against his right leg as he moved. He shifted slightly to compensate so as not to let it slow him down. The gold cord pulled him forward. He knew it led perhaps twenty feet ahead, likely to the left side of the street. He rocked up onto his toes as he walked and spotted the young woman in a glance across the crowd. Her light blue hat bobbed between the people, visible for only a moment, but it was enough. It stood out in the middle of all the gray and black everyone else was wearing at this hour.

Dorrin's path cut through the crowd, and he turned, spun, and hopped right and then left, ever avoiding bumping into or being stepped on by others. She was ten feet ahead now, pausing every few steps to resettle the big sack in her arms. Dorrin's eyes searched her back, and he found her money. She carried it hanging loose in a small bag under her right arm. He was just a few steps behind her when he sensed that she was stopping to juggle the sack again. She turned halfway, as though to look behind her. Dorrin took a brisk step into an alley to his left. That was when hands grabbed his arm, yanking him off balance farther into the alley and shattering his concentration.

He pulled back reflexively and prepared to run, but the hands kept a firm grip. "Skink!" he managed, not sure whether the situation had taken a turn for the better or the worse.

The taller boy snarled at Dorrin and dragged him down the alley. "We've been looking for you. You're late." Dorrin half jogged along, half stumbled. The five purses and pouches banged against his legs with every step.

"I was coming back. I just saw one more-"

"You're coming back now. I'm done having to fetch you every night." Skink shoved Dorrin ahead of him, and Dorrin spotted the girl waiting behind the bins, dressed in rags only slightly cleaner than the ones he and Skink wore.

"Fairy! What are you doing out here?"

She gave him a wry smile and punched his shoulder. "I do get let out on occasion, you know." Her smile dropped, and she fell into stride with the two boys. "Scrounger won't be happy you're late again."

Dorrin knew it was a risk to go after those final three marks, but hopefully the two extra purses he got would prove worth it. Skink grabbed Dorrin's sleeve and yanked him to a rough halt. "How many did you get, anyway?"

Dorrin saw Fairy stare at him pointedly from over Skink's shoulder. She held up two fingers. "Two," Dorrin lied. "I got two." Fairy nodded, relieved.

Skink sneered at him. "So I've outdone his lordship tonight, have I? Look at this." Skink pulled open his dirty coat, and Dorrin saw three small sacks hanging from the inner lining. Dorrin glanced from the sacks to Fairy, but her face was blank now. "What do you have to say for yourself, eh?"

Dorrin looked back to Skink and could smell the bigger boy's sweat. "I... I guess you got me this time," he said.

"Why don't we just count it while we're at it?" Skink shoved Dorrin, and his back slammed against the brick wall of the alley.

Dorrin tried to stammer a response, but Fairy interrupted. "Come on, Skink. We're already late. There'll be time to count when we get back. Let's go."

Skink glared at Dorrin for another instant before giving a curt nod. "Right, let's go."

# ABOUT THE AUTHOR

Jason Dorough is the author of the epic fantasy Teshovar series. Originally from Georgia, Jason now lives in Florida, where he works as a voiceover artist when he's not writing. You can visit him online at JasonDorough.com.

Made in the USA
Columbia, SC
08 January 2024

30081872R00074